# THROUGH-THE-YEAR
# BIBLE
# PUZZLES

by
**Martha Kauffman Coffman**

**STANDARD
PUBLISHING**
Cincinnati, Ohio

Use the King James Version or New International Version.

Scripture quotations marked (NIV) are taken from the HOLY BIBLE, NEW INTERNATIONAL VERSION®. NIV®. Copyright © 1973, 1978, 1984 by International Bible Society. Used by permission of Zondervan Publishing House. All rights reserved.

The Standard Publishing Company, Cincinnati, Ohio
A division of Standex International Corporation

02 01 00 99 98 97 96 95                    5 4 3 2 1

ISBN  0-7847-0320-5

# CONTENTS

# Happy New Year in the Lord

The Bible helps us make New Year's resolutions, but we can make promises to God anytime. If you need help from Paul's writings, turn to 1 Thessalonians 5:12-22 (NIV). Put the answers on the bells.

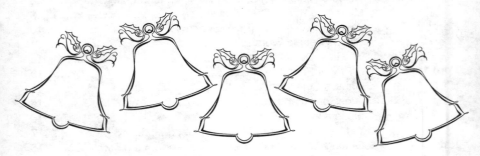

1. __ __ __ __ __ __ __ others who work hard.
2. Live in __ __ __ __ __ with each other.
3. Be __ __ __ __ __ __ __ __ with everyone.
4. Always try to be __ __ __ __ with each other.
5. Be __ __ __ __ __ __ always
6. __ __ __ __ continually.
7. Give __ __ __ __ __ __ in all circumstances.
8. __ __ __ __ everything.
9. __ __ __ __ on to the good.
10. __ __ __ __ __ every kind of evil.

# People In Genesis

How many of these characters from Genesis do you recognize? Circle the ones you know with a pen or pencil. Use another color for the ones you do not know and try to learn about them. They go up, down, across, diagonally, or backwards.

```
A B R A H A M A J R E R
S E S A U Z E S A A E E
I N L G O D T H C M P B
M J O S E P H E O A H E
E A T A M N U R B T R K
O M M R E I S A A C A A
N I A A H A E M V T I H
J N D H S C L Z Y V M X
A E A T U W A B E L S P
P H A R A O H L R E V E
H A H A S E T H Q G O N
E G S C M H N O A H N O
T A U H A M A D I D K C
H R C E L A B A N G A H
F C L L B D R E U B E N
```

| | | | |
|---|---|---|---|
| Abel | Ephraim | Joseph | Rebekah |
| Abraham | Esau | Laban | Reuben |
| Adam | Eve | Leah | Sarah |
| Asher | Gad | Levi | Seth |
| Benjamin | God | Methuselah | Shem |
| Cain | Hagar | Lot | Simeon |
| Cush | Isaac | Noah | Tamar |
| Dan | Jacob | Pharaoh | |
| Enoch | Japheth | Rachel | |

# Winter Weather Words

The words in this puzzle go in different directions like a cold wintry wind. Can you add others to this list?

```
S E A S O N A L W A R N I N G
N O S N O W B O U N D A U P I
O K A S S N O W Y H I G H P C
W I N D Y L E S L I P P E R Y
S U O D R A Z A H R A E L C C
T E M P E R A T U R E S Y I O
O C L O U D I N E S S N T P L
R L O W S F L U R R Y O I A D
M O N A S R A S R C N I L T F
W S A V U E O A T O B T I A R
A E I E B E L O W L A I B O O
T D R A Z Z I L B A D D I O N
C O L D E I S L E E T N S O T
H O N A R N L E S S A O I N E
A M A P O G A L E T A C V N E
```

| | | |
|---|---|---|
| air | flurry | snowbound |
| below | freezing | snowstorm |
| blizzard | gale | snowy |
| clear | seasonal | temperatures |
| closed | high | visibility |
| cloudiness | icy | warning |
| cold | lows | watch |
| cold front | map | wave |
| hazardous | sub zero | windy |
| conditions | sleet | |

# Happy Words

Valentine's Day makes us feel happy when we do things for each other. Find happy words, plus a special scrambled three-word message at the top of the heart. The words go up, down, backward, and diagonally.

```
      E B    M Y           F N D E I R
   D E I F S I T A S     E N C O U R A G E
 L U N N E V A E H G O D Q U I E T S I N G
 I P W J E S U S V M G D E T H G I L E D O
 K L I U R P A R T Y L D E L I C I O U S O
 E A N B U N I T Y K E Q P T H R I L L E D
 X Y N I S Y N N U S E A I T Y D A L G E V
   M I L A F M E R R Y T N E T N O C T S
   H N A E U E I T R E F R E S H A A X L
     G N L N E L O V E R E E H C I A P
       T P L E A S E D W C Y L C Z E
         K C O M F O R T M L E E A
           Y N O M R A H N R C C
             L Y L L O P P A E
             L J O T P E Y
               O L A P H
               J O Y
```

| | | | | |
|---|---|---|---|---|
| appreciate | heaven | play | cheer | harmony | pleased |
| comfort | Jesus | pleasure | content | jolly | quiet |
| delicious | joy | refresh | delighted | jubilant | satisfied |
| encourage | like | sing | fun | love | sunny |
| glee | merry | thrilled | glad | party | unity |
| God | peace | winning | good | | |

# Helpers

Find the names of these important helpers in the puzzle. You may want to surprise some of them by making valentines for them. Hidden in the leftover letters are two words. Draw a red heart around them.

```
F A T H E R A D V I S E R M E I C G G E
R U O V E R S E E R D O C T O R O U R N
I N U R S E C O U N S E L O R Q O I A E
E T E A C H E R L A N D L O R D K D N M
N M A I L C A R R I E R C O A C H E D Y
D T R A I N E R P R I N C I P A L C M G
S U P E R I N T E N D E N T Z I P H O R
E T A M A N A G E R S A D S B N C A T A
C O F F I C E R F L O V E I R S U I H N
R R D E N T I S T G O D E S O T S R E D
E E L D E R P A S T O R G T T R T P R F
T A B C O U S I N U R J R E H U O E Q A
A D O W V C O L L E C T O R E C D R U T
R E S M O T H E R L M B C O R T I S L H
Y R S L E A D E R G R O C E R O A O M E
D B U S D R I V E R A H R N K R N N E R
```

| | | | | |
|---|---|---|---|---|
| adviser | cook | father | leader | principal |
| aunt | counselor | friends | mail carrier | secretary |
| boss | cousin | grandfather | manager | sister |
| brother | custodian | grandmother | mother | superintendent |
| bus driver | dentist | grocer | nurse | teacher |
| chairperson | doctor | guide | officer | trainer |
| coach | elder | instructor | overseer | tutor |
| collector | enemy* | landlord | pastor | |

*Remember: Jesus said, "Love your enemies."

# Match the Kings

How many of these kings can you name without looking up the reference? Can you name other kings?

____ 1. Ruled when Joseph was in Egypt (Genesis 39:1).

____ 2. First king of Israel (1 Samuel 10:20-24).

____ 3. Once a shepherd boy (1 Samuel 16:11-13).

____ 4. The wisest man (1 Kings 3:12).

____ 5. King at age eight (2 Kings 22:1).

____ 6. Ate grass. Later praised God (Daniel 4:33).

____ 7. A Roman king when Jesus was born (Luke 2:1).

____ 8. Wanted to kill Jesus (Matthew 2:13).

____ 9. Almost persuaded to be a Christian (Acts 26:27, 28).

____ 10. Our heavenly king (John 12:13).

a. Nebuchadnezzar  
b. Caesar Augustus  
c. Solomon  
d. Josiah  
e. Pharaoh  

f. Agrippa  
g. Saul  
h. Herod  
i. Jesus  
j. David  

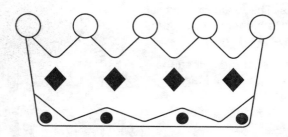

# Jesus' Special Ride

The story of the triumphal entry can be found in Matthew 21, Mark 11, Luke 19, and John 12. How many correct answers can you circle without checking your Bible? Give yourself a grade from 1-10. If you miss more than three read the story.

1. This happening was prophesied by (Abraham, Moses, Zechariah) in the Old Testament.

2. The Mount near Jerusalem where the story began was called: (Herman, Olives, Sinai).

3. The crowd came to Jerusalem to (celebrate the Feast of the Passover, to see a donkey auction, to see the disciples).

4. The story happened (six weeks before Jesus died, in the last week before Jesus died, after He rose from the dead).

5. Jesus sent (five, three, two) disciples to the village to untie a donkey and bring it to Him.

6. Jesus wanted to (buy the donkey, have the disciples ride it, borrow the donkey for himself).

7. The disciples put their (saddle, cloaks, blanket) on the donkey before Jesus sat on it.

8. To honor Jesus, the crowds spread (olive, sycamore, palm) branches on the path where He rode.

9. The crowd cheered and asked who Jesus was. They said He was Jesus of (Bethlehem, Jerusalem, Nazareth).

10. The crowds shouted, "Hosanna to the son of (Joseph, Mary, David)."

SCORE: _____

# Places People Worshiped

Match these Bible people to the places where they worshiped.

1. NOAH set up an altar after he left the _____. (Genesis 8:18-20)

2. JACOB set up a _____. (Genesis 35:14)

3. God appeared to MOSES in a burning _____. (Exodus 3:1-4)

4. SAMUEL was lying down in the _____.(1 Samuel 3:3)

5. DANIEL prayed at his _____. (Daniel 6:10)

6. JONAH prayed inside the big _____. (Jonah 2:1)

7. WISE MEN came to the _____ where Jesus was. (Matthew 2:11)

8. JESUS went to the _____ to pray all night (Matthew 26:36)

9. JESUS read the Scripture in the _____. (Luke 4:16-19)

10. LYDIA and other women prayed by the _____. (Acts 16:13, 14)

11. PAUL and SILAS prayed in _____. (Acts 16:25)

a. garden

b. window

c. prison

d. synagogue

e. stone pillar

f. temple

g. riverside

h. ark

i. house

j. fish

k. bush

# The Last Days for Jesus

Can you arrange these events of the last week before Jesus died and arose again? Find the answers from John 12:12 to 20. The headings at the top of the Bible may help you. Write them on the lines.

**ARRANGE**                    **CORRECT ORDER**

a.  Peter denied the Lord             1. _____

b.  Jesus before Pilate               2. _____

c.  Judas betrayed Jesus              3. _____

d.  Women found an empty tomb         4. _____

e.  Jesus washed His disciples' feet  5. _____

f.  Nicodemus cared for Jesus' body   6. _____

g.  Jesus prayed long to His Father   7. _____

h.  Jesus died on the cross           8. _____

i.  Jesus rode into Jerusalem         9. _____

# A Prayer From the Cross

When Jesus was on the cross, He prayed for those who did not love Him. Can you match the numbers with the letters and write the verse on the line?

```
    a  d  e  f  g  h  i  k  m  n  o  r  t  v  w  y
    1  2  3  4  5  6  7  8  9 10 11 12 13 14 15 16
```

___ ___ ___ ___ ___ ___ ,  ___ ___ ___ ___ ___ ___ ___   ___ ___ ___ ___ ,
 4   1  13  6   3  12       4  11  12  5   7  14   3      13   6   3   9

___ ___ ___   ___ ___ ___ ___   ___ ___   ___ ___ ___   ___ ___ ___ ___
 4  11  12    13   6   3  16     2  11    10  11  13     8  10  11  15

___ ___ ___ ___   ___ ___ ___ ___   ___ ___ ___   ___ ___ ___ ___ ___ .
15   6   1  13    13   6   3  16     1  12   3     2  11   7  10   5

Luke 23:34 (NIV)

# Christ's Suffering

Isaiah 53 foretold how Christ would suffer. Fill in the missing vowels in these "suffering" words from that passage.

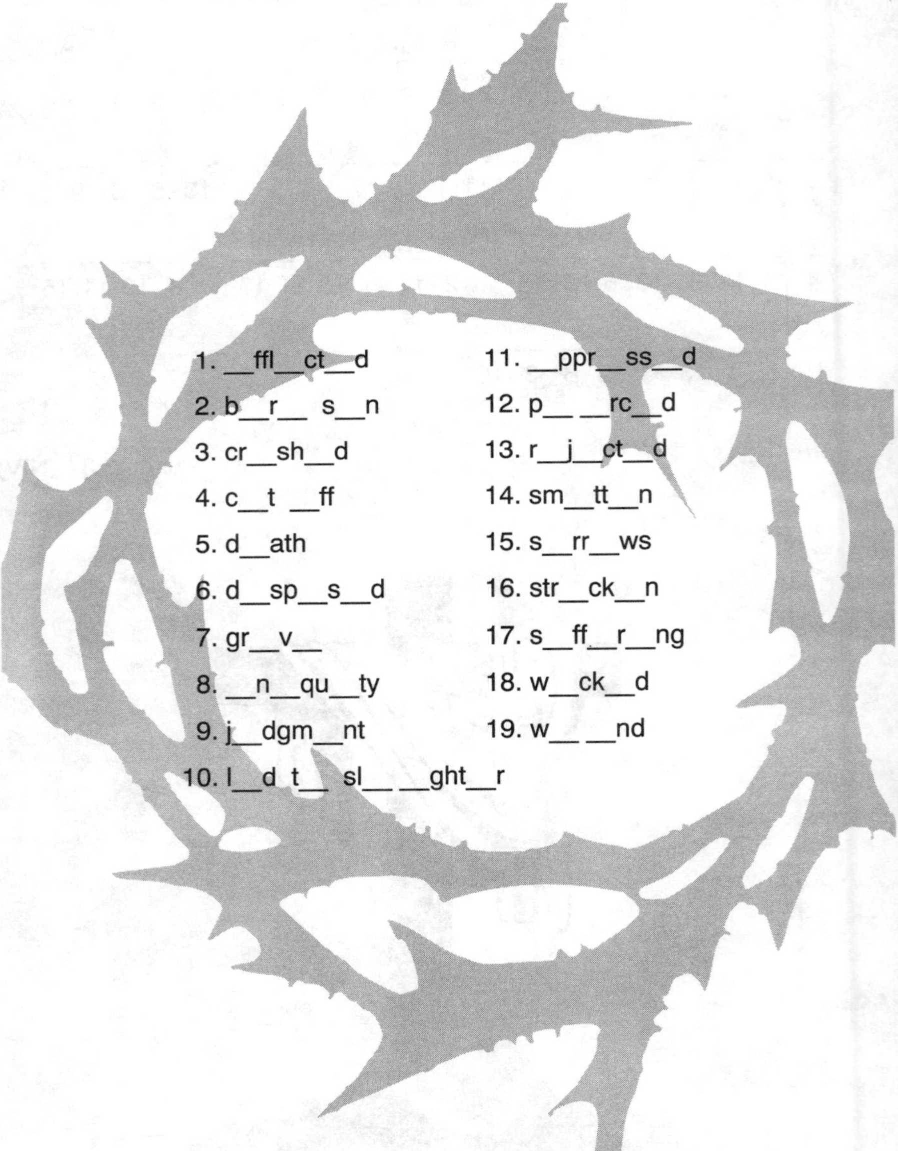

1. __ffl__ct__d
2. b__r__ s__n
3. cr__sh__d
4. c__t __ff
5. d__ath
6. d__sp__s__d
7. gr__v__
8. __n__qu__ty
9. j__dgm__nt
10. l__d t__ sl__ __ght__r

11. __ppr__ss__d
12. p__ __rc__d
13. r__j__ct__d
14. sm__tt__n
15. s__rr__ws
16. str__ck__n
17. s__ff__r__ng
18. w__ck__d
19. w__ __nd

# Cross or Tomb

Put the words for the last days of Jesus on the cross. Place those that took place after the resurrection time by the tomb. Use John 19 and 20 as a guide. Can you add other words?

1. angels
2. blood
3. body
4. bones
5. early morning
6. empty

7. gardener
8. Golgotha
9. hyssop
10. linen found
11. peace
12. Pilate

13. risen
14. seamless garment
15. soldiers
16. stone
17. thieves
18. vinegar

# Make a Word

The first letter of each answer spells an important word for us. Think of other words to go with this important word.

Women got up (1.) _____ in the morning.

They found that an (2.) _____ had rolled away

the (3.) _____ from the (4.) _____ .

It was (5.) _____, because Jesus had

_____ from the dead.

_____

# Trees—Our Helpers

People in Bible times used trees for many reasons. Can you identify the trees with the story or persons?

1. God created many kinds of trees for _____ and other ways to serve the peoples of the world (Genesis 1:12).

2. Adam and Eve ate fruit from the _____ tree in the Garden of Eden (Genesis 3:3).

3. When the Lord appeared to _____, he sat near the big trees by his tent entrance (Genesis 18:1).

4. When visitors came to Abraham, they washed their _____ and rested under a tree (Genesis 18:4).

5. Joshua made a covenant with the people and set it up under an _____ tree (Joshua 24:25, 26).

6. Solomon sent a message to Hiram king of Tyre to send _____ logs to build the temple of the Lord (2 Chronicles 2:3, 4).

7. Zacchaeus wanted to see Jesus and climbed into a _____ tree (Luke 19:4).

8. The crowds put branches of _____ trees along the path to honor Jesus (Matthew 21:8; John 12:13).

# Getting Ready for Heaven

These sentences will remind us to get ready for Heaven. Write the answers next to the numbers. The first letters will tell you the name of a holy day that comes 40 days after Easter.

1. __ __ __ __    The story of Jesus going to Heaven in a cloud is in the first chapter of this New Testament book.

2. __ __ __ __    Jesus came to _____ us from our sins (Matthew 1:21).

3. __ __ __ __    Jesus promised to _____ back (John 14:3).

4. __ __ __    When Jesus comes again, every _____ shall see Him (Revelation 1:7).

5. __ __ __ __ __ __ __ __    We brought _____ into this world, and it is certain we can carry _____ out (1 Timothy 6:7).

6. __ __ __ __ __    Another name for a Christian is _____ (Romans 1:7).

7. __ __ __ __ __ __ __ __    If we do not obey God's Word, we cannot _____ the kingdom of God (Galatians 5:21).

8. __ __ __ __    Children shall _____ their parents (Ephesians 6:1).

9. __ __ __ __    We shall sing a _____ song in Heaven (Revelation 5:9).

Write the name of the day

here _____ Day.

This year the date is

_____ _____, 19_____.

# Mother's Day Bouquet

Each of these flower names is a compound word. Can you match it to the right clue?

1. Mom is more precious than this kind of stick. _____

2. You can put these two on the table for lunch. _____

3. This flower names a Christmas plant, but blooms in summer. _____

4. You can paper your living room with this one. _____

5. This flower is always well-behaved. _____

6. This could be the brightest flower you have. _____

7. Find this flower on a bird. _____

8. The sweetest flower to climb the fence. _____

9. The name sounds like the quick bite of an angry animal. _____

10. You might hear its sound at school time. _____

11. If you stumble over this, you can get hurt. _____

12. A mitt for a kit? _____

Choices: a. bluebell; b. bloodroot; c. buttercup; d. foxglove; e. goldenrod; f. hollyhock; g. honeysuckle; h. larkspur; i. primrose; j. snapdragon; k. sunflower; l. wallflower.

# Special Bible Mothers

Mothers of famous persons are not always recognized as they should be. Can you unscramble their names and match them with their well-known children?

| MOTHERS | CHILDREN |
|---|---|
| 1. Bethalize _____ (Luke 1:13) | Esau and Jacob |
| 2. Vee _____ (Genesis 4:1, 2) | Eunice |
| 3. Nuicee _____ (2 Timothy 1:2, 5) | Jesus |
| 4. Soil _____ (2 Timothy 1:5) | Obed |
| 5. Beekhar _____ (Genesis 25:20-26) | John the Baptist |
| 6. Debojech _____ (Exodus 6:20) | Cain and Abel |
| 7. Charle _____ (Genesis 35:24) | Timothy |
| 8. Haras _____ (Genesis 21:1-3) | Moses and Aaron |
| 9. Thur _____ (Ruth 4:13, 17) | Isaac |
| 10. Army _____ (Matthew 1:20, 21) | Joseph |

# Bible Memorials

A country often erects memorials for its people or events that made history. God wants His memorials to be in the hearts of the people who serve Him. Write the answers on the heart.

1. _____ wrote the memory of defeating the Amalekites (Exodus 17:14).

2. The Children of Israel came out of _____ (Exodus 18:1).

3. _____ will be remembered for putting perfume on Jesus (John 11:2).

4. The coming out of Egypt will be a lasting _____ (Exodus 12:17).

5. The memory of the _____ will be a blessing (Proverbs 10:7).

6. Twelve stones from the Jordan River were to represent the 12 tribes of _____ (Joshua 4:4-7).

7. The names of the sons of Israel were engraved on _____ ephod (Exodus 28:11, 12).

8. A book of remembrance was written for those who feared and honored the _____ (Malachi 3:16).

9. God will remember our _____ no more (Hebrews 8:12).

The first letters of each answer spells "Memorials."

Memorial

# Bible Singers

Can you match the special singers with the Bible events?

1. _____ sang when he saw God's power in leading the Children of Israel (Exodus 15:1).

2. When _____ saw what God did, she danced and sang with tambourines (Exodus 15:21).

3. After _____ and _____ sang, the land had peace for 40 years (Judges 5:1).

4. _____ sang about Cush and thanked God (Psalm 7).

5. _____ sang when she was to become the mother of the Christ child (Luke 1:46).

6. _____ sang after John the Baptist was born (Luke 1:67).

7. The _____ of Jesus sang a hymn before Jesus went to the Mount of Olives and Gethsemane (Mark 14:16, 17, 26).

8. _____ and _____ prayed and sang hymns after being thrown into prison (Acts 16:25).

a. Zechariah; b. Miriam; c. Mary; d. Moses; e. Paul, Silas; f. David; g. disciples; h. Deborah, Barak.

# Children's Day

Children had an important part in home life in Bible times. Solomon wrote a proverb that helps children to do well. Write the verse with the code. Can you memorize it?

CODE: A = 1; B = 2; C = 3; D = 4; E = 5; F = 6; G = 7; H = 8; I = 9; J = 10; K = 11; L = 12; M = 13; N = 14; O = 15; P = 16; Q = 17; R = 18; S = 19; T = 20; U = 21; V = 22; W = 23; X = 24; Y = 25; Z = 26.

__ __ __ __   __   __ __ __ __ __   __ __   __ __ __ __ __
5  22 5  14   1    3  8  9  12 4    9  19   11 14 15 23 14

__ __   __ __ __   __ __ __ __ __ __ __ ,   __ __
2  25   8  9  19   1  3  20 9  15 14 19      2  25

__ __ __ __ __ __ __   __ __ __   __ __ __ __ __ __ __
23 8  5  20 8  5  18   8  9  19   3  15 14 4  21 3  20

__ __   __ __ __ __ __   __ __ __ __ __ .
9  19   16 21 18 5      1  14 4   18 9  7  8  20

__ __ __ __ __ __ __ __   20:11 (NIV).
16 18 15 22 5  18 2  19

# Fathers Who Heard God Speak

The Bible tells about fathers who received special messages and commands from God. Write them on the blanks.

ACROSS:
1. "Where are you?" God asked (Genesis 3:9).
3. After he talked to God, he set up a stone pillar (Genesis 35:13, 14).
5. He and his family were to take charge of the tent or tabernacle (Numbers 18:1-3).
7. God promised him a wise and discerning heart (1 Kings 3:12).

DOWN:
1. Make his family a great nation (Genesis 12:1, 2).
2. Told to build an ark (Genesis 6:13, 14).
4. Commanded not to go to Egypt (Genesis 26:1, 2).
6. God called from a burning bush for him to be a leader (Exodus 3:4).
8. When he had many problems, God asked him many questions (Job 38).

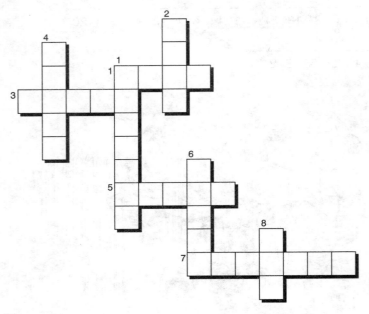

We can receive messages from God by _____.

# Pentecost Quiz

Many people don't know much about the Holy Day called Pentecost. How do you rate? After you take the quiz, give yourself a letter grade. If you need more help, read the story in the Bible. A calendar, dictionary, or encyclopedia may also give you information.

1. The story of Pentecost is found in ____.
   a. Genesis 2; b. Matthew 2; c. Acts 2

2. Pentecost is celebrated because _____.
   a. Jesus went to Heaven; b. the Holy Spirit came; c. Jesus was baptized.

3. Pentecost is _____ days from Easter.
   a. 40; b. 50; c. 10

4. Pentecost is _____ days after Ascension Day.
   a. 40; b. 50; c. 10

5. Another name for Pentecost is _____.
   a. Advent; b. Passover; c. Feast of First Fruits

6. The person who preached the first Pentecost sermon was _____.
   a. Paul; b. Jesus; c. Peter

7. He preached mostly from the _____.
   a. Old Testament; b. New Testament; c. book of Acts

8. Pentecost first came in the form of a _____.
   a. violent wind; b. rainbow; c. dew

9. The number of persons who accepted the message and were baptized on the day of Pentecost was _____.
   a. 200; b. 3000; c. 12

10. After the people were baptized, they _____.
    a. went to tell the merchants; b. begged in the streets of Jerusalem; c. spent much time in prayer.

# A Whale of Words

These words belong to the story of Jonah. (To refresh your memory, read the thirty-second book of the Bible.) As you find the words, can you think what part each one has in the story?

afraid
anger
asleep
believed
calm
city
country
cried
die
displeased
down

earth
fainted
fare
fish
flee
forty
go
God
gourd
Hebrew

holy
I
Jonah
Joppa
king
left
Lord
lots
mariners
mountains

Nineveh
obeyed
overboard
perish
prayed
repent
robe
sackcloth
sacrifice
sea
shadow

ship
storm
Tarshish
thanksgiving
thousand
under
violence
vow
waters
waves
weeds

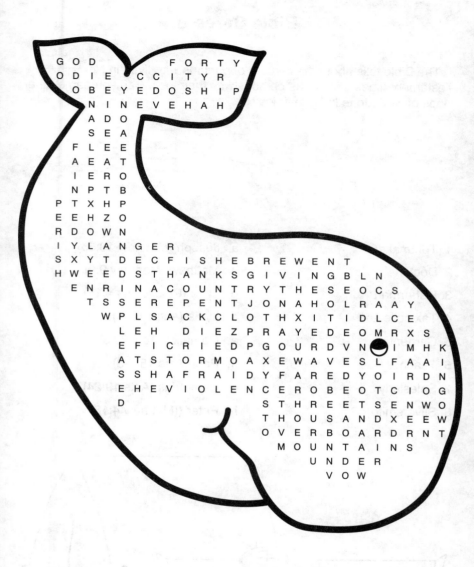

# Bible Careers

The Bible tells about the careers of persons who lived in New Testament times. Match the persons with their jobs. Can you name other kinds of work done in Bible times?

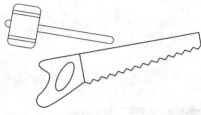 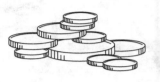

1. Tentmaker

2. Doctor

3. Fisherman

4. Tax collector

5. Carpenter

6. Teacher

7. Saleslady

8. Silversmith

a. Joseph (Matthew 13:55)

b. Matthew (Matthew 9:9)

c. Luke (Colossians 4:14)

d. Lydia (Acts 16:14)

e. Gamaliel (Acts 22:3)

f. Paul (Acts 18:1-3)

g. Demetrius (Acts 19:24)

h. Peter ((Matthew 4:18)

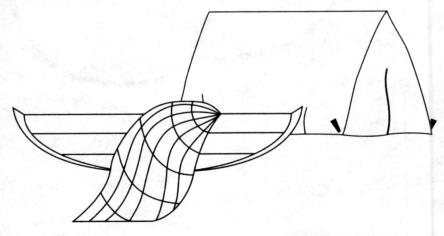

# They Called Him, "Lord"

The book of John tells about persons who called Jesus, "Lord." Match the verses (NIV) with the right people. Can you find others in the Bible who called Him, "Lord"?

1. A blind man (9:38)____

2. Mary and Martha (11:3)____

3. Jesus (13:14)____

4. Philip (14:8)____

5. Mary Magdalene (20:18)____

6. Thomas (20:28)____

7. Peter (21:16)____

8. John the Baptist (1:23)____

a. "My Lord and my God!"

b. "I have seen the Lord!"

c. "Lord, I believe."

d. "Lord, the one you love is sick."

e. "Lord, show us the Father."

f. "Yes, Lord, you know that I love you."

g. "Now that I, your Lord and Teacher, have washed your feet."

h. "Make straight the way for the Lord."

# Beatitudes Quiz

Jesus pronounced blessings on different groups of people in Matthew 5:1-12. We call these verses Beatitudes. How many can you match without checking your Bible? "Blessed are . . .

## PERSONS

___ 1. The poor in spirit

___ 2. Those who mourn

___ 3. The meek

___ 4. Those who hunger and thirst after righteousness

___ 5. The merciful

___ 6. The pure in heart

___ 7. The peacemakers

___ 8. Those who are persecuted because of righteousness

___ 9. You when people insult you, persecute you and falsely say all kinds of evil against you because of me.

## BLESSINGS

a. They will be filled.

b. They will see God.

c. Theirs is the kingdom of heaven.

d. They will be called sons of God.

e. Rejoice and be glad, because great is your reward in heaven.

f. Theirs is the kingdom of heaven.

g. They will be shown mercy.

h. They will inherit the earth.

i. They will be comforted.

# Church Musical Words

You may use these words in your church music programs. Can you fill the crossword sections with the words below?

**ACROSS:**
1. High or low range of a sound - _____
2. Music sung without instruments - _____
3. Phrases sung at the end of each stanza - _____
4. Sung during a formal service - _____

**DOWN:**
5. Song for Christmas or Easter - _____
6. Sung as an elaborate solo - _____
7. Group of persons who do special singing - _____
8. Song of grief for a funeral - _____
9. Song also used to quiet children - _____
10. Repeated musical phrases - _____

chant; lullaby; refrain; carol; a capella; dirge; pitch; aria; hymn; choir

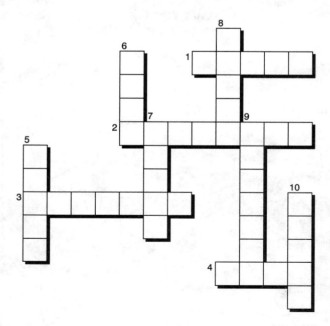

# Persons Paul Helped

Paul preached in many places and helped these people become Christians. Can you match the people with their descriptions?

1. Titus_____
2. Silas_____
3. Aquila_____
4. Timothy_____
5. Barnabas_____
6. Lydia_____
7. Onesimus_____
8. Priscilla_____
9. Crispus_____
10. Elymas_____

a. Saleslady who loved to pray (Acts 16:14)
b. Slave who needed help (Philemon 1:10)
c. Came from Italy (Acts 18:1-3)
d. His evil spirit left him (Acts 13:8-11)
e. An elder in Crete (Titus 1:5)
f. Sang with Paul in prison (Acts 16:25)
g. Chief ruler of the synagogue (Acts 18:8)
h. Young helper with good report (Acts 16:1, 2)
i. Helped her husband make tents (Acts 18:1-3)
j. Went on the first missionary journey with Saul (Paul)—(Acts 13:2, 3)

# My Body Belongs to God

The Bible tells us important things about our bodies, so that we will take care of them. List some of your good habits.

1. We praise God because we are _____ and _____ made (Psalm 139:14).

2. Because of what Jesus did for us, we should offer our bodies as _____ of righteousness (Romans 6:13).

3. Our body is the _____ of the Holy Spirit (1 Corinthians 6:19).

4. Because we are bought with a _____, we shall honor God with our bodies (1 Corinthians 6:20).

5. Our bodies are sacred and God's _____ lives within us (1 Corinthians 3:16, 17).

6. We shall not let _____ reign in our mortal bodies (Romans 6:12).

7. Can you name things the Bible says will defile our bodies?
   _____

   Are there other things?
   _____

8. When we are tempted to think or do evil, we can remember David's prayer (Psalm 51:10). "_____ in me a clean heart, O God; and _____ a right spirit within me."

**Good Habits**

1. _____    4. _____

2. _____    5. _____

3. _____    6. _____

# Readers in the Bible

In Bible times, because there were so few copies, the Book of the Law was read to people from handwritten scrolls. Think about how you learned to read and have a Bible of your own. Use your Bible to match the person with the story.

1. _____ read the Book to the adults and children (Joshua 8:34, 35).

2. _____ and his helpers read The Book of the Law clearly, so that everyone could understand it (Nehemiah 8:8).

3. When the Book was read, the _____ cried when they heard it (Nehemiah 8:9).

4. _____ interpreted handwriting on the wall for King Belshazzar (Daniel 5:12).

5. After the Book was found in the temple, Shaphan read it to King _____ (2 Chronicles 34:18).

6. As _____ was reading the Book, King Jehoiakim threw all its leaves into the fire (Jeremiah 36:23).

7. _____ stood up in the synagogue to read the Book (Luke 4:16).

8. _____ joined a man in a chariot to help him understand what he was reading (Acts 8:30, 31).

9. _____ wrote to Timothy and told him to read the Scriptures in public (1 Timothy 4:13).

10. _____ wrote that people will be blessed if they read Revelation (Revelation 1:1, 3).

Jesus; Joshua; Philip; Daniel; Jehudi; John; Paul; people; Ezra; Josiah.

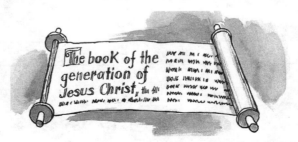

# Writing in the Bible

Bible characters wrote in many different ways. Place their names on the grid. As you match the writing with the characters, think of the many ways you write.

## ACROSS:

2. _____ wrote on two tablets of stone (Deuteronomy 5:22).
3. The _____ wrote commandments on doorframes for their children (Deuteronomy 6:4, 9).
4. _____ wrote a title for Jesus on the cross (John 19:19).
5. The wicked Queen _____ signed her husband's name with his (king's) seal (1 Kings 21:7, 8).
7. _____ wrote a book to prove that Jesus was the Christ, the Son of God (John 20:31).

## DOWN:

1. The Israelites watched _____ copy the Law of Moses on stone (Joshua 8:32).
4. _____ wrote to Timothy for him to bring the scrolls and parchments (2 Timothy 4:13).
5. _____ told Baruch to write with ink on a scroll (Jeremiah 36:18).
6. _____ wrote on the ground with his finger (John 8:6).

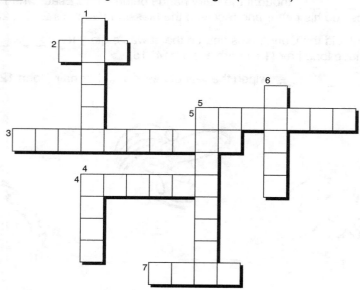

# Hair

The Bible speaks about hair. Can you fill in the blanks?

1. Jesus told His _____ that the hairs of their heads were numbered (Matthew 10:5, 30).

2. The beauty of the old men is the _____ hair (Proverbs 20:29).

3. When his hair was shaven _____'s strength left him (Judges 16:19).

4. _____'s hair weighed two hundred shekels (about five pounds) when it was cut (2 Samuel 14:26).

5. Three men came out of a fiery _____ without having one hair singed (Daniel 3:26, 27).

6. _____ thought the hairy hands belonged to Esau, when Jacob deceived his father and received the blessing (Genesis 27:22, 23).

7. Paul told the Corinthians church that it was a glory for a _____ to have long hair (1 Corinthians 11:14, 15).

8. _____ wiped the feet of Jesus with her hair (John 12:3).

# Say "No" to Temptation

These Bible verses (NIV) will help us when we are tempted. Find words that go with each letter in "temptation."

1. "Whatever is true . . .T ____ about such things" (Philippians 4:8).

**T** _ _ _ _

2. "Turn from E____ and do good" (Psalm 34:14).

**E** _ _ _ _

3. If we sin we can pray. "God, have M ____ on me, a sinner" (Luke 18:13).

**M** _ _ _ _ _

4. "P____ continually" (1 Thessalonians 5:17).

**P** _ _ _ _

5. A prayer when in doubt: "T____ me your way, O Lord" (Psalm 27:11).

**T** _ _ _ _ _

6. "A___ every kind of evil" (1 Thessalonians 5:22)

**A** _ _ _ _

7. It helps us to remember that Christ was ____ in every way we are, "yet was without sin" (Hebrews 4:15).

**T** _ _ _ _ _ _ _

8. "____ will call on him as long as I live" (Psalm 116:2).

**I**

9. "Children, O____ your parents in the Lord" (Ephesians 6:1).

**O** _ _ _

10. "A good N____ is more desirable than great riches" (Proverbs 22:1).

**N** _ _ _

# Which Season?

The Bible tells us many things about the seasons. The answers are: autumn, spring, summer, and winter. How many can you do without looking up the verses?

1. "As long as the earth endures, . . . _____ and _____ will never cease" (Genesis 8:22, NIV).

2. God promised to send rain in both _____ and _____ (Deuteronomy 11:14).

3. The heat of _____ can sap strength (Psalm 32:4).

4. The _____ rains shall cover the Valley of Baca with pools (Psalm 84:6).

5. A wise son gathers crops in _____ (Proverbs 10:5).

6. To give honor to a fool is like having snow in _____ (Proverbs 26:1).

7. Jesus told His disciples that when the fig tree sprouts its leaves, they will know that _____ is near (Luke 21:29, 30).

8. When Paul and his ship crew sailed in a dangerous storm, they hoped to reach Crete before _____ (Acts 27:12).

9. The farmer waits patiently for the _____ and _____ rains to make the crops grow (James 5:7).

# Bible Study

We need these words to study the Bible. They go, up, down, across, and diagonally. Can you list other words?

```
C S N O I T S E U Q S P S D E
H P R O P H E T S T E A B I E
A Y R T E O P W E E L R R C C
P V E R S E T N A A T A E T N
T E S T A M E N T C S G V I A
E R Y R O T S I H H I R O O D
R S P S A L M S Y I P A R N R
D I E L B I B K A N E P P A O
R O A N S W E R R G A H U R C
O N Q U E S S A P J S D N Y N
W U E Z I R O M E M E T I M O
G E N E A L O G Y M A S U A C
X H I I T O R Y O G A M U D E
Y G O L T E N E G D P P A S Y
S T N E M D N A M M O C S I N
```

| | | | |
|---|---|---|---|
| answer | genealogy | poetry | teaching |
| Bible | God | pray | testament |
| chapter | history | prophets | unit |
| concordance | Jesus | proverbs | verse |
| commandments | maps | psalms | version |
| dictionary | memorize | questions | word |
| epistles | paragraph | study | |

# To Help You in School

This verse will help you do right in school. Cross out the first and every other letter to discover the message. Then write the message on the lines.

```
W L N E L T A Y A O B U S R H L O I
J G R H E T V S P H Z I Q N D E V B
L E D F S O T R U E S M L E B N, A T
O H W A N T G T D H L E M Y V M K A
E Y A S L E P E K Y M O R U S R W G
A O N O A D F D L E N E X D L S H A
J N X D L P A R I A R I F S N E U Y
L O S U X R H F Z A M T V H K E C R
B I V N L H C E X A C V W E Z N.
```

Matthew 5:16 (NIV)

_____

_____

_____

# Be Thankful

This Bible verse helps you to thank God. Can you find the code and write it on the lines? Try to memorize it.

__ __ __ __,    __ __ __    __ __    __ __ __ __    __ __ __
3  15  13  5    12  5  19    20  18    18  9  14  7    6  15  17

__ __ __    __ __    __ __ __    __ __ __ __;    __ __ __
10  15  24    19  15    19  8  5    12  15  17  4    12  5  19

__ __    __ __ __ __ __  __ __ __ __ __  __ __    __ __ __
20  18    18  8  15  20  19    1  12  15  20  4    19  15    19  8  5

__ __ __ __  __ __  __ __ __  __ __ __ __ __ __ __ __ __.
17  15  3  11    15  6    15  20  17    18  1  12  21  1  19  9  15  14

__ __ __  __ __  __ __ __ __  __ __ __ __ __ __
12  5  19    20  18    3  15  13  5    2  5  6  15  17  5

__ __ __  __ __ __ __  __ __ __ __ __ __ __ __ __ __ __
8  9  13    22  9  19  8    19  8  1  14  11  18  7  9  21  9  14  7

__ __ __  __ __ __ __ __  __ __ __  __ __ __ __
1  14  4    5  23  19  15  12    8  9  13    22  9  19  8

__ __ __ __ __  __ __ __  __ __ __ __
13  20  18  9  3    1  14  4    18  15  14  7

(__ __ __ __ __    95:1, 2, NIV).
16  18  1  12  13

*Let's all give thanks*

# Christmas ABC's

A_ _ _ _ _ _        Sang to announce Jesus' birth.
B_ _ _ _ _ _ _ _    Where Jesus was born.
C_ _ _ _ _ _        Another name for Jesus.
D_ _ _ _ _          Bethlehem, city of _____
E_ _ _ _ _ _ _ _    Cousin of Mary and mother of John
                      the Baptist.
F_ _ _ _ _ _        Grazed in the fields the night of
                      Jesus' birth.
G_ _                Planned the birth of Jesus.
H_ _ _ _ _          King who wanted to kill Jesus.
I_ _                Place that had no room for Joseph
                      and Mary.
J_ _ _ _ _          Husband of Mary.
K_ _ _              The wise men called Jesus this.
L_ _ _              Wrote the story of the shepherds
                      and the angels.
M_ _ _ _            Mother of Jesus.
N_ _ _ _ _ _ _ _    Hometown of Jesus and his family.
O_ _ _ _ _ _ _      The wise men _____ Jesus gifts.
P_ _ _ _ _ _ _      King Herod called these leaders to
                      learn of Jesus' birthplace.
Q_ _ _ _            Describes the night, before the
                      angels announced Jesus' birth.
R_ _ _ _ _ _ _      We _____ (are glad) that Jesus was
                      born.
S_ _ _ _            Guided the wise men to Jesus.
T_ _ _ _ _ _ _ _ _ _  Joseph and Mary took a pair of
                      of these to the temple.
U_ _ _ _ _–         Teachers in the temple were
                      amazed at Jesus' _____ as he
                      was growing up (Luke 2:47).
_ _ _ _ _ _ _ _ _   "Behold, a _____ shall be with child
V_ _ _ _ _ _          and shall bring forth a son"
                      (Matthew 1:23).
W_ _ _ _ _ _ _      Came to worship Jesus and brought
                      gifts to him.
X_ _ _ _ _ _ _      The wise men rejoiced with _____
                      great joy.
Y_ _ _              "For unto ____ is born this day"
                      (Luke 2:11).
Z_ _ _ _ _ _ _ _    Father of John the Baptist.

# Christmas Carols

How many of these carols can you do without looking at a hymnal? Try to sing each one as you do them. Then list other carols.

1. Away in a _____

2. O Little Town of _____

3. _____ to the World

4. O Come, Little _____

5. We _____ Kings

6. Silent _____

7. O _____, All Ye Faithful

8. The _____ Noel

9. Hark! the Herald _____ Sing

10. While _____ Watched

# His Name Is John

We learn much about Zechariah, Elizabeth, and their son, John in Luke 1. Arrange the answers in the blanks around "John the Baptist."

1. John prepared the way for _____ (1:17).
2. King when John was born _____ (1:5).
3. Father of John _____ (1:13).
4. An _____ appeared to his parents (1:11).
5. Mother of John _____ (1:13).
6. They had no _____ before John (1:7).
7. Many will _____ at John's birth (1:14).
8. After John's _____ his father said "Praise
9. be to the Lord God of _____" (1:68)
10. Zechariah's _____ was heard (1:13).
11. John was to be filled with the Holy _____ (1:15).
12. He shall not drink ____ (1:15).
13. Zechariah could not _____ until John was born (1:20).
14. On a writing _____ Zechariah wrote, "His name is John." (1:63).

```
        J _ _ _
    _ _ O _
    _ _ H _ _ _ _
    _ N _ _ _

_ _ _ _ _ _ T _
    _ H _ _ _ _ _
    _ E _ _ _ _

    _ B _ _ _
  _ _ A _ _
    _ P _ _ _ _
_ _ _ _ T _ _
  _ I _ _
    _ S _ _ _
_ _ _ _ T
```

# People Who Lived at Jesus' Birth

Can you match the persons with their part in the time of Jesus' birth? You can find the answers in Luke 1 and 2.

\_\_\_ 1. King of Judea

\_\_\_ 2. Forerunner of Jesus

\_\_\_ 3. Cousin of His mother

\_\_\_ 4. Prophetess

\_\_\_ 5. He would not die until he saw Jesus.

\_\_\_ 6. Sent out a tax notice

\_\_\_ 7. Husband of His mother's cousin

\_\_\_ 8. Virgin who gave birth to God's son

\_\_\_ 9. Husband of the virgin who gave birth to Jesus

PERSONS:
a. Zechariah; b. Caesar Augustus; c. Anna; d. Elizabeth; e. Herod; f. Simeon; g. John the Baptist; h. Mary; i. Joseph.

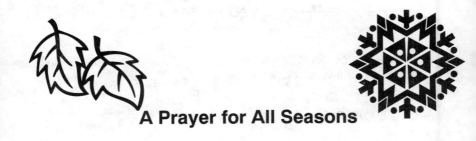

# A Prayer for All Seasons

Many prayers in the Bible are suitable for us today. Unscramble the words as you write the verse on the lines. You may also print them on a large paper to hang in your room.

YAM HET DORWS FO YM THOUM DAN TEH TIMEDNATIO FO MY TEARH EB SEALPGNI NI ROUY HISGT, O ROLD, YM CORK DAN MY MEEDERRE. MALSP 19:14.

_____ _____ _____ ___ ___ _____ _____

___ _____ _____ ___ ___ _____

_____ ___ _____ ___ _____, ___ _____,

___ ___ ___ ___ _____.

_____ 19:14 (NIV)

# Answers

*Happy New Year in the Lord:* 1. Respect. 2. Peace. 3. Patient. 4. Kind. 5. Joyful. 6. Pray. 7. Thanks. 8. Test. 9. Hold. 10. Avoid.

*Match the Kings:* 1. e; 2. g; 3. j; 4. c; 5. d; 6. a; 7. b; 8. h; 9. f; 10. i

*Jesus' Special Ride:* 1. Zechariah. 2. Olives. 3. Celebrate the Feast of the Passover. 4. in the last week. 5. two. 6. borrow the donkey for himself. 7. cloaks. 8. Palm. 9. Nazareth. 10. David.

*Places People Worshiped:* 1. h; 2. e; 3. k; 4. f; 5. b; 6. j; 7. i; 8. a; 9. d; 10. g; 11. c.

*The Last Days for Jesus:* i, e, g, c, a, b, h, f, d

*Christ's Suffering:* 1. Afflicted, 2. bore sin, 3. crushed, 4. cut off, 5. death, 6. despised, 7. grave, 8. iniquity, 9. judgment, 10. led to slaughter, 11. oppressed, 12. pierced, 13. rejected, 14. smitten, 15. sorrows, 16. stricken, 17. suffering, 18. wicked, 19 wound.

*Cross or Tomb:* CROSS: blood, body, bones, Golgotha, hyssop, Pilate, seamless garment, soldiers, thieves, vinegar. TOMB: angels, early morning, empty, gardener, linen found, peace, risen, stone.

*Make a Word:* 1. Early 2. Angel 3. Stone 4. Tomb 5. Empty 6. Risen

*Trees—Our Helpers:* 1. fruit; 2. middle; 3. Abraham; 4. feet; 5. oak; 6. cedar; 7. sycamore; 8. palm.

*Getting Ready for Heaven:* 1. Acts; 2. Save; 3. Come; 4. Eye; 5. Nothing; 6. Saint; 7. Inherit; 8. Obey; 9. New

*Mother's Day Bouquet:* 1. e; 2. c; 3. f; 4. l; 5. i; 6. k; 7. h; 8. g; 9. j; 10. a; 11. b; 12. d.

*Special Bible Mothers:* 1. Elizabeth; 2. Eve; 3. Eunice; 4. Lois; 5. Rebekah; 6. Jochebed; 7. Rachel; 8. Sarah; 9. Ruth; 10. Mary

*Bible Memorials:* 1. Moses. 2. Egypt. 3. Mary. 4. Ordinance. 5. Righteous. 6. Israel. 7. Aaron's. 8. Lord. 9. Sins

*Bible Singers:* 1. d; 2. b; 3. h; 4. f; 5. c; 6. a; 7. g; 8. e.

*Fathers Who Heard God Speak:* **Across:** 1. Adam. 3. Jacob. 5. Aaron. 7. Solomon. **Down:** 1. Abraham. 2. Noah. 4. Isaac. 6. Moses. 8. Job.

*Pentecost Quiz:* 1. c; 2. b; 3. b; 4. c; 5. c; 6. c; 7. a; 8. a; 9. b; 10. c.

*Bible Careers:* 1. f; 2. c; 3. h; 4. b; 5. a; 6. e; 7. d; 8. g.

*They Called Him, "Lord":* 1. c; 2. d; 3. g; 4. e; 5. b; 6. a; 7. f; 8. h.

*Beatitudes Quiz:* 1. c or f; 2. i; 3. h; 4. a; 5. g; 6. b; 7. d; 8. c or f; 9. e.

*Church Musical Words:* **Across:** 1. Pitch. 2. A capella. 3. Refrain. 4. Hymn. **Down:** 5. Carol. 6. Aria. 7. Choir. 8. Dirge. 9. Lullaby. 10. Chant.

*Persons Paul Helped:* 1. e; 2. f; 3. c; 4. h; 5. j; 6. a; 7. b; 8. i; 9. g; 10. d.

*Readers in the Bible:* 1. Joshua; 2. Ezra; 3. people; 4. Daniel; 5. Josiah; 6. Jehudi; 7. Jesus; 8. Philip; 9. Paul; 10. John.

*Writing in the Bible:* **Across:** 2. God. 3. Israelite. 4. Pilate. 5. Jezebel. 7. John. **Down:** 1. Joshua. 4. Paul. 5. Jeremiah. 6. Jesus.

*Hair:* 1. disciples; 2. gray; 3. Samson; 4. Absalom; 5. furnace; 6. Isaac; 7. woman; 8. Mary.

*Say "No" to Temptation:* 1. Think; 2. Evil; 3. Mercy; 4. Pray; 5. Teach; 6. Avoid; 7. Tempted; 8.I; 9. Obey; 10. Name.

*Which Season?:* 1. summer and winter; 2. autumn and spring; 3. summer; 4. autumn; 5. summer; 6. summer; 7. summer; 8. winter; 9. autumn and spring;

*To Help You in School:* Let your light shine before men, that they may see your good deeds and praise your father in heaven. Matthew 5:16.

*Be Thankful:* Code: a-1; b-2; c-3; d-4; e-5; f-6; g-7; h-8; i-9; j-10; k-11; l-12; m-13; n-14; o-15; p-16; r-17; s-18; t-19; u-20; v-21; w-22; x-23; y-24.

*Christmas ABC's:* angels, Bethlehem, Christ, David, Elizabeth, flocks, God, Herod, inn, Joseph, king, Luke, Mary, Nazareth, offered, priests, quiet, rejoice, star, turtledoves, understanding, virgin, wise men, exceeding, you, Zechariah.

*Christmas Carols:* 1. Manger; 2. Bethlehem; 3. Joy; 4. Children; 5. Three; 6. Night; 7. Come; 8. First; 9. Angels; 10. Shepherds.

*His Name Is John:* 1. Jesus. 2. Herod. 3. Zechariah. 4. Angel. 5. Elizabeth. 6. Children. 7. Rejoice. 8. Birth. 9. Israel. 10. Prayer. 11. Spirit. 12. Wine. 13. Speak. 14. Tablet

*People Who Lived at Jesus' Birth:* 1. e; 2. g; 3. d; 4. c; 5. f; 6. b; 7. a; 8. h; 9. i.

*A Prayer for All Seasons:* May the words of my mouth and the meditation of my heart be pleasing in your sight, O Lord, my Rock and my Redeemer. Psalm 19:14.